Playalong Songs

By Jane Sebba

Illustrated by Steve Smallman

Hamish Hamilton
London

First published 1986
Published by Hamish Hamilton Children's Books
Garden House 57-59 Long Acre, London WC2E 9JZ.

Copyright © 1986 by Jane Sebba.

Illustrations copyright © 1986 Hamish Hamilton Ltd.
All Rights Reserved.

British Library Cataloguing in Publication Data
Sebba, Jane
Playalong songs.
1. Children's songs, English — Texts
I. Title
784.6'2405 PZ8.3

ISBN 0-241-11653-8

Typeset by Words and Music Graphics, Southend, Essex.
Printed in Great Britain by
St. Edmundsbury Press, Bury St. Edmunds, Suffolk.

For my sister Nicky who is my inspiration — this book is her fault!

Many adults and children have contributed advice and ideas to
this book. I would like to thank all of them, in particular
Jonathan Dove, who has added sparkle to the project with his
musical expertise and his magical fingers.

My special thanks also go to Dot Fraser, Linda and Paul Read,
Jeremy Sams, Rosalie Sebba, Katharine Verney, and Fiona
and John York.

A cassette tape of all these songs is available. It is called
Playalong Songs and is released by Pickwick on Children's Series
Ditto 10515. In case of difficulty in obtaining the cassette,
please contact Hamish Hamilton Children's Books.

Contents

Preface

All the songs in this book have been sung and played by the children in the ILEA primary school where I work. These children are aged 3-11.

The songs fall into 3 categories: action songs, those using percussion instruments, and stories.

The songs are designed to involve the whole class in some activity as well as singing.

The action songs and those using percussion instruments speak for themselves. They are intended to be versatile, so wherever possible use any actions, and any instruments.

After we have sung the 'story' songs (such as City Safari) we play them on tuned percussion.

If you have a few tuned percussion instruments, try out this simple and effective system where children all play one note on the ringed beats of each bar .

G A B C D E				E F♯ G				G G♯ A B				B C D				D E			
City Safari				City Safari				City Safari				City Safari				City Safari			
① 2 ③ 4				① 2 ③ 4				① 2 ③ 4				① 2 ③ 4				① 2 ③ 4			
G	B	C	D	G	F♯	E	F♯	G	B	G	A	B	B	C	D	D	D	E	D
G	B	C	D	G	F♯	E	F♯	G	B	G	A	B	B	C	D	D	D	E	D
A	D	G	E	E	F♯	G	E	A	A	G	G♯	C	D	B	B	E	D	D	E
A	D	G	G	E	F♯	G	G	A	A	G	G	C	D	B	B	E	D	D	D

A set of parts for City Safari looks like this.

Make each part into a work card. In the top right hand corner are the names of the notes used on that card. Two children can read from one card but each will need his own set of notes on an instrument. Make duplicates of cards as necessary.

The children read across the card and play each note in turn on the ringed beats.

Make sure the children are used to feeling the first beat of the bar. Do a variety of clapping, tapping heads, etc. before playing the instruments. We pat our knees to the music on the first beat as a matter of course before playing, regardless of how experienced the children are.

The system involves everybody in an activity which can be graded according to the individual's ability.

Throughout the book the figure ♩. ♪ is not to be taken literally but as the jazz convention for ♩ ³ ♪

This means that ♩. ♪ ♩. ♪ (difficult)

is actually played ♩ ³ ♪ ♩ ³ ♪ (easy)

Playalong

1. Join in with the action —
   Join in with the game.

   You can sing a song,
   You can play along,
   It's never the same.

   Clap your hands,
   Clap your hands.
   Do it again,
   Do it again.

2. Join in with the action —
   Join in with the game.

   You can sing a song,
   You can play along,
   It's never the same.

   Snap your fingers,
   Snap your fingers.
   Do it again,
   Do it again.

3. Join in with the action —
   Join in with the game.

   You can sing a song,
   You can play along,
   It's never the same.

   Click your tongue,
   Click your tongue.
   Do it again,
   Do it again.

(last time) You joined in the action —
   You joined in the game.

8

1. Clap your hands,   Clap your hands.
2. Snap your fing - ers,   Snap your fing - ers.
3. Click your tongue,   Click your tongue.

F7   B♭   B♭m6

Do it a - gain.   Do it a - gain.

Repeat ad lib

A7   Dm   A7   Dm   G7   C7   G7   C7

Last time

You joined in the act - ion.   You joined in the game.

F6   D♭7   Gm7   C7   F

Instruments:

Use any action or any instrument, changing the words and rhythm as necessary :

bar 9: Play the tam-bou-rine

Ideas for performance:

A soloist or small group chooses an action to perform or an instrument to play for one verse.
They can sing a solo in bars 9-12, then everyone joins in from bars 13-16.

Ideas for teachers:

Teach the rhythm of bars 10, 12, 14 and 16 before you sing the song.

Say "Clap your hands",

then clap

and ask the children to copy.

9

Together They Make a Pair

1. One hand on this side and
   One hand on that side,
   Together they make a pair.
       They're just like each other but
       One's here and the other is there.

   Shake the left one in the air.
   Now the right one to make it fair.
   Then we can shake them both at once.
       They're just like each other but
       One's here and the other is there.

2. One foot on this side and
   One foot on that side,
   Together they make a pair.
       They're just like each other but
       One's here and the other is there.

   Shake the left one in the air.
   Now the right one to make it fair.
   Then we can shake them both at once.
       They're just like each other but
       One's here and the other is there.

3. One arm on this side and
   One arm on that side,
   Together they make a pair.
       They're just like each other but
       One's here and the other is there.

   Shake the left one in the air.
   Now the right one to make it fair.
   Then we can shake them both at once.
       They're just like each other but
       One's here and the other is there.

A song for both sides of your body.

Ideas for performance :

Choose any part of the body which has
a right and a left (arm, leg, thumb, knee,
hip, cheek, etc.)

11

Any Way You Like

1. Pick up a drum and make it play
   So it goes boom boom boom boom.
   Play it again so we can listen.

   Play it very fast,
   Play it very slow,
   Play it loud,
   Start it soft and make it grow.
   Play it near your foot,
   Play it near your ear.
   Now play it any way you like
   So we can hear.

2. Pick up a triangle and make it play
   So it goes ting ting ting ting.
   Play it again so we can listen.

   Play it very fast,
   Play it very slow.
   Play it very loud,
   Start it soft and make it grow.
   Play it near your foot,
   Play it near your ear.
   Now play it any way you like
   So we can hear.

3. Pick up some cymbals and make them play
   So they go clash clash clash clash.
   Play them again so we can listen.

   Play them very fast,
   Play them very slow.
   Play them very loud,
   Start it soft and make it grow.
   Play them near your foot,
   Play them near your ear.
   Now play them any way you like
   So we can hear.

4. Pick up a tambourine and make it play
   So it goes clink clink clink clink.
   Play it again so we can listen.

   Play it very fast,
   Play it very slow.
   Play it very loud,
   Start it soft and make it grow.
   Play it near your foot,
   Play it near your ear.
   Now play it any way you like
   So we can hear.

Last verse:

Pick up your instrument and make it play — etc.

13

The song introduces a few set rhythms and then gives the children a chance to try out some rhythms of their own.

Instruments: Drum
Triangle
Cymbals
Tambourine

Use any other instruments as well, changing the words and rhythm.

Pick up a tri-an-gle and make it play...

You can use any number of each instrument.

Everybody plays in the last verse.

Ideas for teachers:

Teach the rhythms for playing fast, slow, etc., by clapping hands before you sing the song. Clap each rhythm and then ask the children to copy.

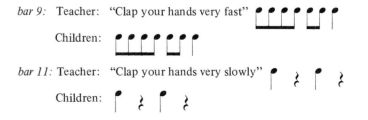

bar 9: Teacher: "Clap your hands very fast"

Children:

bar 11: Teacher: "Clap your hands very slowly"

Children:

Wobbly Tooth

I've got a wobbly tooth.
I've got a tooth that's loose.
I'm going to wobble it and wobble it
around and about —
Until it comes out.

    I'm going to wobble it this way
    And wobble it that way,
    I'll wobble it on Friday and
    I'll wobble it on Saturday.
    I'll give it a tug and
    I'll give it a tap.
    I'll wobble it until I've got a great big gap.

I had a wobbly tooth.
I had a tooth that was loose.
I wobbled it and wobbled it
around and about —
Until it came out.

16

wob-bled it and wobbled it a - round and a - bout. un-til it came out.

C   F   F♯dim   G   C

Tuned percussion parts (First and last 8 bars)

C D F F♯ G A				B C				D D♯ E F				F F♯ G				G A			
Wobbly tooth				Wobbly tooth				Wobbly tooth				Wobbly tooth				Wobbly tooth			
① 2 ③ 4				① 2 ③ 4				① 2 ③ 4				① 2 ③ 4				① 2 ③ 4			
C	G	C	G	C	B	C	B	E	D♯	E	D♯	G	G	G	G	G	G	G	G
C	A	D	G	C	C	C	B	E	E	D	D	G	G	F♯	G	G	A	A	G
C	C	F	F♯	C	C	C	C	E	E	F	D♯	G	G	F	F♯	G	G	A	A
G	G	C	C	B	B	C	C	D	D	E	E	G	G	G	G	G	G	G	G

Touch Your Shoe

1. Clap your hands — tap your thighs —
   Clap your hands — blink your eyes —
   Clap your hands — reach up high
   And try to touch the sky.

   Bring your hands down, touch your shoe
   And now choose something else to do.

2. Nod your head — tap your thighs —
   Nod your head — blink your eyes —
   Nod your head — reach up high
   And try to touch the sky.

   Bring your hands down, touch your shoe
   And now choose something else to do.

3. Stamp your feet — tap your thighs —
   Stamp your feet — blink your eyes —
   Stamp your feet — reach up high
   And try to touch the sky.

   Bring your hands down, touch your shoe,
   (last time) There's nothing else to do.

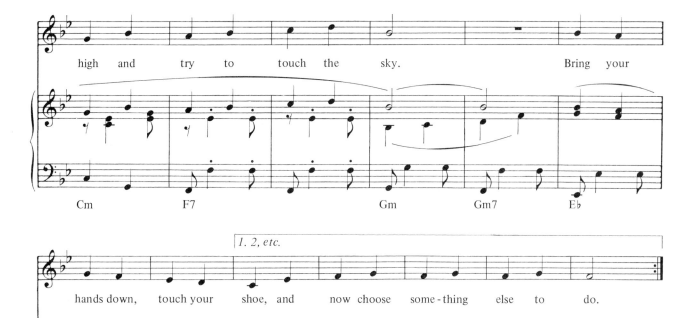

high and try to touch the sky. Bring your

Cm   F7   Gm   Gm7   E♭

1. 2, etc.

hands down, touch your shoe, and now choose some-thing else to do.

G7   Cm   E♭m   B♭   B♭m   F7sus4   F7

Last time

shoe, there's noth-ing else to do.

rit . . . .

E♭m   B♭   F7   B♭

An action-packed song.

The words and actions:

> "Tap your thighs,
> Blink your eyes,
> Reach up high
> And try to touch the sky."

remain constant throughout each verse, but any action can precede them.

Ideas for performance:

The children choose a new action for each verse,
and a soloist or small group sings and performs it,
while everyone joins in with 'tap your thighs', 'blink your eyes', etc.

19

That Would Make Me Smile

1. Would you like to choose an instrument
   To play for a little while?

   > I'd like to play the wood blocks —
   > That would make me smile.

2. Would you like to choose an instrument
   To play for a little while?

   > I'd like to play the tambourine —
   > That would make me smile.

3. Would you like to choose an instrument
   To play for a little while?

   > I'd like to play the drum —
   > That would make me smile.

20

The children can choose which instrument to play.

Instruments: Wood blocks
Tambourine
Drum
Maracas

Use any other instrument as well, and change the words and rhythm:

I'd like to play the tam - bour - ine . . .

I'd like to play the drum . . .

I'd like to play the ma - ra - cas . . .

You could even use glockenspiels or recorders in this song.
If you do, let the children keep to the notes G A B D E in bars 9 - 16.

Use any number of each instrument.

Ideas for performance:

A soloist or small group chooses an instrument.
Everyone else sings the question and the soloist sings the answer.
During bars 9 - 16, the soloist plays to a minim beat.
Some children might like to improvise their own rhythms in these eight bars.

The Triangle Song

This is a triangle,
Look and you'll see
One edge, another edge,
And a third edge makes three.

This is a triangle,
Look and you'll see
We can imagine all the
Things it can be.

Add a big red bobble here;
Now it's a hat on a clown.

Add a broomstick and a cat;
Now it's a witch with a frown.

Draw some waves from the deep blue sea;
Now it's the sail on a boat.

Make it of metal and give it a tap;
A triangle plays a nice note.

This is a triangle,
Look and you'll see
One edge, another edge,
And a third edge makes three.

This is a triangle,
Look and you'll see
We can imagine all the
Things it can be.

22

What can a triangle become? Here are some ideas.

You will need these 'props'.
They should be made of card,
and must be big enough to be seen clearly.

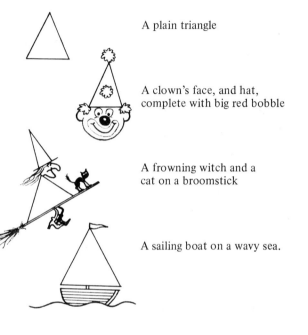

A plain triangle

A clown's face, and hat,
complete with big red bobble

A frowning witch and a
cat on a broomstick

A sailing boat on a wavy sea.

Instruments: At least one triangle. You could use more.

Ideas for performance:

Everyone sings the first and last sixteen bars,
and traces the outline in the air of the triangle in bars 5 - 7.

Choose soloists or small groups for these activities:

1. To display the plain triangle in bars 1 - 16,
   and trace its outline in bars 5 - 7.
2. To sing bars 17 - 23, and display the clown.
3. To sing bars 25 - 31, and display the witch.
4. To sing bars 33 - 39, and display the boat.
5. To sing bars 41 - 47, and to play the triangle
   from bar 48 to the end of the song.

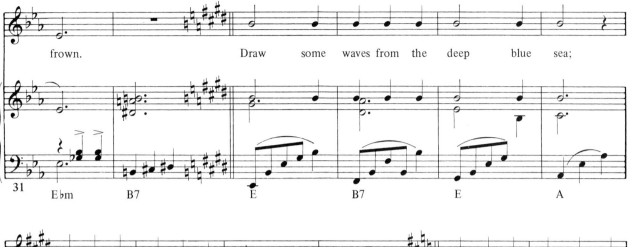

frown. Draw some waves from the deep blue sea;

Now it's the sail on a boat. Make it of met - al and

give it a tap; a tri - ang - le plays a nice note.

Tuned percussion parts:

First (and last) 16 bars only.

D E G A				B C♯ D			
Triangle song				Triangle song			
① 2 3				① 2 3			
D	A	D	G	D	C♯	D	D
D	D	E	A	D	B	B	C♯
D	A	D	G	D	C♯	D	D
D	D	A	D	D	B	C♯	D

D E				F♯ G			
Triangle song				Triangle song			
① 2 3				① 2 3			
D	E	D	D	F♯	G	F♯	G
D	D	E	E	F♯	F	G	G
D	E	D	D	F♯	G	F♯	G
D	D	E	D	F♯	F	G	F♯

G♯ A B			
Triangle song			
① 2 3			
A	A	A	B
A	G♯	B	A
A	A	A	B
A	G♯	A	A

Here is a Drum

A: Here is a drum.
Here is a drum.
Here is a drum.
and it's your turn to play it.
If you've got something musical to say
then don't delay it,
and use the drum to say it.

B: Here is a drum.
Here is a drum.
Here is a drum
and it's my turn to play it.
I've got something musical to say,
I won't delay it,
I'll use the drum to say it.

Here is a drum and it's my turn to play it. I've got something mu-si-cal to say, I won't de-lay it; I'll

F   Gm7   C7   B♭   C7   Am7   D7

use the drum to say it.

Gm7   C7   F   A   E7

A   E7   Amaj7   Am7

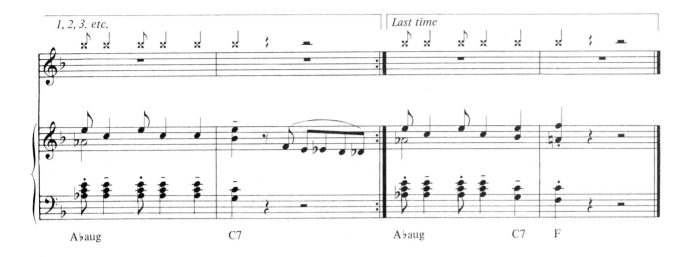

Instruments:

Use any instruments, changing the words and rhythm:

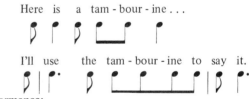

Ideas for performance:

A soloist or small group chooses an instrument to play.
The rest of the children sing the first eight bars.
The soloist or small group sing the next eight bars,
and then play their instruments as written for the remaining eight bars.

Some children may like to improvise their own rhythms in the last section.

Clap-Happy

1. It's a clap - happy song.
    If you're happy clap along.
    Clap once, twice,
    Clap a rhythm that sounds nice,
    It's a clap - happy song.

2. It's a snap - happy song
    If you're happy snap along.
    Snap once, twice,
    Snap a rhythm that sounds nice,
    It's a snap - happy song.

3. It's a tap - happy song.
    If you're happy tap along.
    Tap once, twice,
    Tap a rhythm that sounds nice,
    It's a tap - happy song.

28

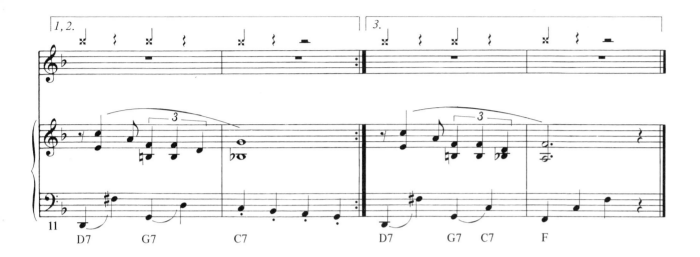

An easy-going song to clap, snap and tap along to.

Ideas for teachers:

Teach the set rhythms of bars 2, 4 and 5 before you sing the song.

(bar 2) :   Say   "Clap   a - long"

and clap

then ask the children to copy.

Some children might like to improvise their own rhythm "that sounds nice" in bars 9 - 12.

Boom–Ting

1. Boom - ting - boom - ting
   Listen to the sound:
   Boom - ting - boom - ting
   Look what we have found.
   A drum and a triangle to help us with the
      song so
   Boom - ting all day long.

2. Ting - click - ting - click
   Listen to the sound:
   Ting - click - ting - click
   Look what we have found.
   A triangle and wood block
      to help us with the song so
   Ting - click all day long.

3. Click - clash - click - clash
   Listen to the sound:
   Click - clash - click - clash
   Look what we have found.
   Wood block and cymbals
      to help us with the song so
   Click - clash all day long.

4. Clash - boom - clash - boom
   Listen to the sound:
   Clash - boom - clash - boom
   Look what we have found.
   Cymbals and a drum
      to help us with the song so
   Clash - boom all day long.

Instruments: Drum
                    Triangle
                    Wood blocks
                    Cymbals

Use any number of each instrument.

Use other instruments as well and change the words and the rhythm:

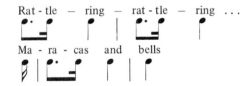

Rat - tle — ring — rat - tle — ring . . .

Ma - ra - cas and bells

Ideas for performance:

The children sit in a circle or line with the instruments in front of them. They should sit in the order that the instruments will be used.

Verse 1: Drums and triangles play as written in the music.

Verse 2: Triangles and wood blocks replace drums and triangles.

Verse 3: Wood blocks and cymbals replace triangles and wood blocks.

The song continues until the drums (or first instruments) are used again.

Faces and Laces

1. On my shoes are a pair of laces,
   That's how the shoes stay on.
   On my shoes are a pair of laces,
   That's how the shoes stay on.
      But you and I have both got faces;
      Faces stay on without the laces.
   Isn't it odd how the
   Bits of your body stay on.

2. On my jacket there's a zip,
   That's how the jacket stays on.
   On my jacket there's a zip,
   That's how the jacket stays on.
      But you and I have both got lips;
      And lips stay on without the zips.
   Isn't it odd how the
   Bits of your body stay on.

3. On my belt there is a buckle,
   That's how the belt stays on . . .
      But you and I have both got knuckles;
      Knuckles stay on without the buckles . . .

Fa - ces stay on with - out the la - ces. Is - n't it odd how the bits of your bo - dy stay
Lips stay on with - out the zips, Is - n't it odd how the bits of your bo - dy stay

A7   D7   G   C   G   D7

1. - 5.   6.

on.
on.

G   D7   G

4. On my badge there is a pin,
   That's how the badge stays on . . .
      But you and I have both got chins;
      And chins stay on without the pins . . .

5. On my satchel there are straps,
   That's how the satchel stays on . . .
      But you and I have both got laps;
      And laps stay on without the straps . . .

6. On my chain there is a clip,
   That's how the chain stays on . . .
      But you and I have both got hips;
      And hips stay on without the clips . . .

Imaginative artists could have fun illustrating the words.

Ideas for performance:

Use the actual articles (lace-up shoes, a zip-up jacket, a belt, etc)
to demonstrate each verse, and point to the appropriate part of the body.

G A B♭ B C D F				F F♯ G				G A B♭ B				B C C♯ D				C D E♭ E			
Faces and laces				Faces and laces				Faces and laces				Faces and laces				Faces and laces			
①2③4				①2③4				①2③4				①2③4				①2③4			
G	B	C	G	G	F♯	G	G	G	B	G	G	B	B	C	B	D	D	E	D
A	D	G	G	G	F♯	G	G	G	A	G	G	C	C	B	B	E	D	D	D
G	B	C	G	G	F♯	G	G	G	B	G	G	B	B	C	B	D	D	E	D
A	D	G	G	G	F♯	G	G	G	A	G	G	C	C	B	B	E	D	D	D
F	F	B♭	B♭	F	F	F	F	A	A	B♭	B♭	C	C	D	D	E♭	E♭	D	D
A	A	D	D	G	G	F♯	F♯	A	A	A	A	C♯	C♯	D	D	E	E	C	C
G	C	D	D	G	G	G	F♯	G	G	G	A	B	C	B	C	D	E	D	D
G	C	G	G	G	G	G	G	G	G	G	G	B	C	B	B	D	E	D	D

33

Standing in the Ring

1. Look at me. Look at me,
   I'm standing in the middle of the ring.
   I can clap my hands and
   I can sing.

      Look at Lisa. Look at Lisa,
      She's standing in the middle of the ring.
      She can clap her hands and
      She can sing.

2. Look at me. Look at me,
   I'm standing in the middle of the ring.
   I can nod my head and
   I can sing.

      Look at Tom. Look at Tom,
      He's standing in the middle of the ring.
      He can nod his head and
      He can sing.

3. Look at me. Look at me,
   I'm standing in the middle of the ring.
   I can stamp my feet and
   I can sing.

      Look at Matthew. Look at Matthew,
      He's standing in the middle of the ring.
      He can stamp his feet and
      He can sing.

For children who love to be in the spotlight.

Ideas for performance:

The children sit on the floor in a circle.
A soloist stands in the middle of the circle and chooses an action.
He or she sings the verse, and performs the action in bar 6.
The rest of the children then sing the verse, incorporating the
soloist's name in bar 1, and changing the rhythm if necessary.

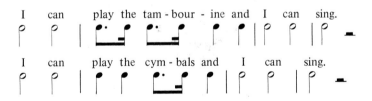

Look   at   Li - sa.   Look   at   Li - sa,   she's   stand - ing . . .

This time everyone performs the action in bar 6.

The soloist returns to sit in the circle.
A new soloists chooses a different action, and goes to the middle of the ring
to perform.

Ideas for teachers:

As well as different actions, (tap my knees, nod my head, etc.) use
instruments.
Change the words and rhythm:

I   can   play the tam - bour - ine and   I   can   sing.

I   can   play the cym - bals and   I   can   sing.

City Safari

1. There's a zebra crossing
   On the zebra crossing.
   There's a zebra crossing the road.
       Look left, look right,
         First it's black, then it's white.
   There's a zebra crossing the road.

2. There's a cat's eye shining
   At the shiny cat's eye.
   There's a cat's eye shining in the lane.
       Look left, look right,
         First it's dark, then it's bright.
   There's a cat's eye shining in the lane.

3. There's a yellow lion
   On the yellow line.
   There's a yellow lion by the kerb.
       Look left, look right,
         Be polite or it'll bite.
   There's a yellow lion by the kerb.

4. There's a big gnu roundabout
   The big new roundabout.
   A big gnu roundabout the town.
       Look left, look right,
         Don't ignore him; say "G'night".
   There's a big gnu roundabout the town.

left, look right; first it's black, then it's white; there's a zeb - ra cross - ing the
first it's dark, then it's bright; there's a cat's eye shin - ing in the
be pol - ite or it - 'll bite; there's a yel - low li - on by the
don't ig - nore him, say "g'-night" there's a big gnu round - a - bout the

Am7   D7   G   E7   Am7   D

1, 2, 3.   4.

road.   town.
lane.
kerb.

G   G

This is a song that lends itself to being acted out in a number of different ways.

Imaginative artists could produce some amusing illustrations for the song.

Tuned percussion parts

G A B C D E				E F♯ G				G G♯ A B				B C D				D E			
City Safari				City Safari				City Safari				City Safari				City Safari			
① 2 ③ 4				① 2 ③ 4				① 2 ③ 4				① 2 ③ 4				① 2 ③ 4			
G	B	C	D	G	F♯	E	F♯	G	B	G	A	B	B	C	D	D	D	E	D
G	B	C	D	G	F♯	E	F♯	G	B	G	A	B	B	C	D	D	D	E	D
A	D	G	E	E	F♯	G	E	A	A	G	G♯	C	D	B	B	E	E	D	E
A	D	G	G	E	F♯	G	G	A	A	G	G	C	D	B	B	E	E	D	D

37

Lolly on a Stick

1. A lolly on a stick is a very nice thing to lick.
   A lolly on a stick is a very nice thing to lick.
   > The first lick is good
   > And the next lick is better
   > But the chunk at the end is the best
   > So get a

   Lolly on a stick — it's a very nice thing to lick.

2. You can bite off the top and nibble right down
   the sides.
   You can bite off the top and nibble right down
   the sides.
   > The first lick is good
   > And the next lick is better
   > But the chunk at the end is the best
   > So get a

   Bite off the top and nibble right down the sides.

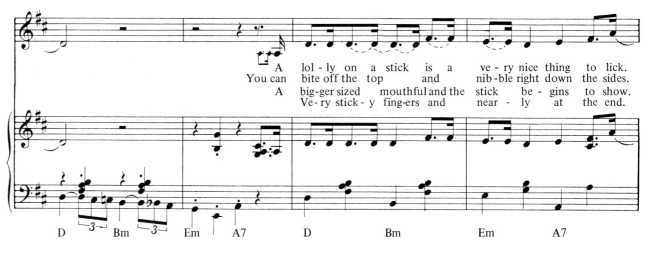

It's a Secret

Can you keep a secret?
Can you keep a secret?
We mustn't let our secret out. (Sh . . .)
We won't even tell you what our
Secret song is about.

It's not about a tree that's tall,
It's not about a bee that's small.
It's not about a house that's wide.
A hundred metres from side to side.

We can keep a secret,
We can keep a secret,
We haven't let our secret out. (Sh . . .)
We won't even tell you what our
Secret song is about.
(Sh . . .)

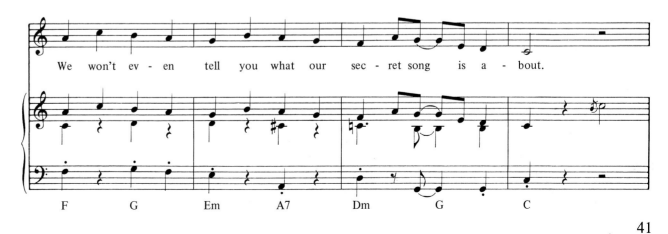

41

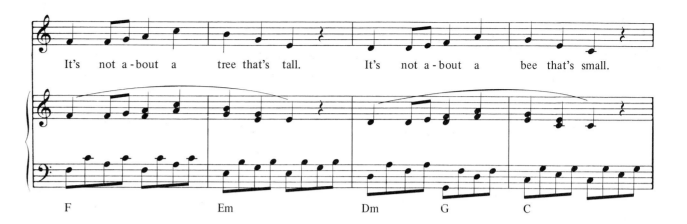

It's not a-bout a tree that's tall. It's not a-bout a bee that's small.

F   Em   Dm   G   C

It's not a-bout a house that's wide - A hun-dred met-res from side to side.

F   Em   D7   G

We can keep a sec-ret, We can keep a sec-ret, We have-n't let our sec-ret out. Sh!

C   Dm G C   Dm G C   Dm G C

We won't ev - en tell you what our sec - ret song is a - bout. Sh!

F G Em A7 Dm G C

Who can keep a secret?

Ideas for performance:

Ask the children if they can think of other things that are tall, small and wide. Substitute these in place of a tree, a bee, and a house for variety.

Tuned percussion parts (First and last 8 bars)

C D E F G A				A B C				C C♯ D E				E F				G A		
It's a secret				It's a secret				It's a secret				It's a secret				It's a secret		
① 2 ③ 4				① 2 ③ 4				① 2 ③ 4				① 2 ③ 4				① 2 ③ 4		
C	G	C	G	C	B	C	B	C	D	C	D	E	F	E	F	G	G	G	G
C	G	C	C	C	B	C	C	C	D	C	C	E	F	E	E	G	G	G	G
F	G	E	A	C	B	B	A	C	D	E	C♯	F	F	E	E	A	G	G	A
D	G	C	C	C	B	C	C	D	D	C	C	F	F	E	E	A	G	G	G

Copyclap

1. Clap your hands together
   when you hear this sound:
   Clap your hands together
   when you hear this sound:

2. Click your fingers together
   when you hear this sound:
   Click your fingers together
   when you hear this sound:

3. Blink your eyes together
   when you hear this sound:
   Blink your eyes together
   when you hear this sound:

44

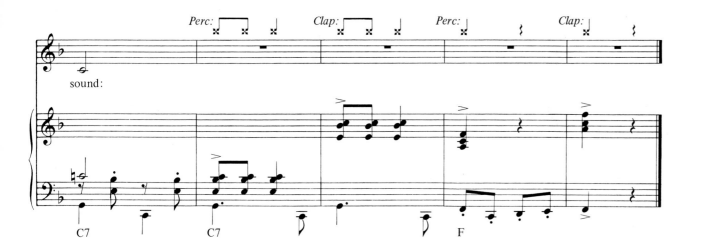

sound:

C7   C7   F

A song which involves instruments leading and actions following.

Instruments:

You can use any instruments (and any actions).
Change the words and rhythm:

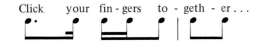

Click   your   fin - gers   to - geth - er . . .

Ideas for performance:

A soloist or small group chooses an instrument to play
and decides which action should follow the instrument.
The rest of the children perform the action.

The song continues until there are no more instruments – or actions – left,
and everyone has played an instrument.

Ideas for teachers:

A more complicated version of this would be to try some combinations:

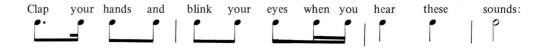

Clap   your   hands   and   blink   your   eyes   when   you   hear   these   sounds:

After the song is finished, see if the children can remember what to do
when they hear each instrument.

One-Man Band

1. Play a rhythm on the drum —
   Sing the song and you'll become
     a one-man band
     and
   Hands'll begin to clap —
   Feet'll begin to tap —
     Very very soon
     Your friends'll know the tune and
     Somebody will want to join your band.

2. Play a rhythm on the tambourine —
   Play a rhythm on the drum —
   Sing the song and you'll become
     a two-man band
     and
   Hands'll begin to clap —
   Feet'll begin to tap —
     Very very soon
     Your friends'll know the tune and
     Somebody will want to join your band.

3. Play a rhythm on the wood blocks —
   Play a rhythm on the tambourine —
   Play a rhythm on the drum —
   Sing the song and you'll become
      a three-man band
      and
   Hands'll begin to clap —
   Feet'll begin to tap —
      Very very soon
      Your friends'll know the tune but
(last time) There's no-one left who wants to
      join your band.

Instruments: Drum
                   Tambourine
                   Wood blocks

Use as many other instruments as necessary.
Use any number of each instrument, and sing
"four-man band" or "eighteen-man band" as
appropriate.

47

Ideas for performance:

Verse 1: The drum plays in bars 2, 5 and 6.
Everyone claps hands in bar 8
and taps feet in bar 10.

Verse 2: The tambourine plays in bar 18.
The drum plays in bar 2.
Tambourine and drum play in bars 5 and 6
Everyone claps hands in bar 8
and taps feet in bar 10.

Verse 3: The wood block plays in bar 20
The tambourine plays in bar 22
The drum plays in bar 2
Wood block, tambourine and drum play
in bars 5 and 6
Everyone claps hands in bar 8
and taps feet in bar 10.

The song continues in this way, adding another
instrument for each verse, until everyone has
joined in on an instrument.

In the last verse sing:
"There's no-one left who wants to join your band!"

Ideas for teachers:

Teach the rhythms for bars 2, 5 and 6, 8, 10 before
you sing the song.

bar 2   Say "Play a rhythm on the   drum",

then clap

The children copy the words and rhythm.

bars 5 & 6   Say "One - man band"

then clap

bar 8   Say "Hands'll begin to clap".

then clap

bar 10   Say "Feet'll begin to tap",

then tap

48

If You're Feeling Discontented

1. If you're very very keen
   To play the tambourine
   Then play it — play it —

   If you're very very keen
   To play the tambourine
   Then play it — play it —
   Chorus

   If you're feeling discontented
   And to play an instrument'd
   Cheer you up and make your day,
   Then take a *tambourine* and play away.

2. If you'd like to play the drum
   Because you're feeling glum
   Then play it — play it —

   Chorus

3. If you'd like to hear a crash
   And make the cymbals clash
   Then play them — play them

   Chorus

4. If you like a little ting
   The triangle will sing
   So play it — play it —
   Chorus

5. If you'd like to make a click
   The wood blocks do the trick
   So play them — play them —
   Chorus

6. If we want to make a band
   Our instruments are grand
   So play them — play them —
   Chorus

feel - ing dis-con-ten-ted and to play an inst - ru-ment-'d cheer you up and make your day, then
then

take a tam-bour-ine and play a - way.
take a big bass drum and play a - way.

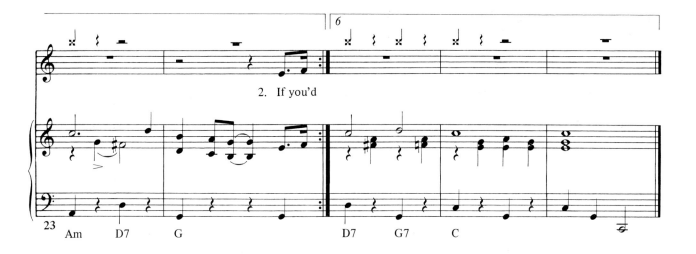

2. If you'd

Am　　D7　　G　　　　　　D7　　G7　　C

A song to cheer you up.

Instruments:　　Tambourine
　　　　　　　　　Drum
　　　　　　　　　Cymbals
　　　　　　　　　Triangle
　　　　　　　　　Wood blocks
Any number of each instrument may be used.

Ideas for performance:

In verses 1 - 5 a soloist or small group of children play as directed in the song.
The other children could pretend they are playing the appropriate instrument
and mime the action with the soloist.

Everyone joins in to sing the last verse:
　　　　　　　"Then take your instrument and play away."

Some children might like to improvise their own rhythms in bars 17 - 24.

That Awful Afternoon

1. I had to be there at 3 o'clock.
   I had to be there at 3 o'clock.
   I had to be there at 3 o'clock
   On that awful afternoon.

2. I had to be there at 3 o'clock.

   I knocked very loudly at the door.
   I knocked very loudly at the door.
   I knocked very loudly at the door
   On that awful afternoon.

3. I had to be there at 3 o'clock.
   I knocked very loudly at the door.

   I walked inside and I sat down.
   I walked inside and I sat down.
   I walked inside and I sat down
   On that awful afternoon.

4. I had to be there at 3 o'clock.
   I knocked very loudly at the door.
   I walked inside and I sat down.

   I trembled as I waited there.
   I trembled as I waited there.
   I trembled as I waited there
   On that awful afternoon.

Percussion: (different for each verse)

1. had to be there at 3 o' clock.
2. knocked ve - ry loud - ly at the door.
3. walked in - side and I sat down.
4. tremb - led as I wait - ed there.
5. heard the mach-ine make a dread - ful noise.
6. went next door when I heard the bell.
7. op-ened my mouth and he poked a - round.

had to be there at 3 o' clock.
knocked ve - ry loud - ly at the door.
walked in - side and I sat down.
tremb - led as I wait - ed there.
heard the mach-ine make a dread - ful noise.
went next door when I heard the bell.
op-ened my mouth and he poked a - round.

I

D

had to be there at 3 o' clock.
knocked ve - ry loud - ly at the door.
walked in - side and I sat down.
tremb - led as I wait - ed there.
heard the mach-ine make a dread - ful noise.
went next door when I heard the bell.
op-ened my mouth and he poked a - round.

On that

D7   G   Gm6

5. I had to be there at 3 o'clock.
    I knocked very loudly at the door.
    I walked inside and I sat down.
    I trembled as I waited there.

    I heard the machine make a dreadful noise.
    I heard the machine make a dreadful noise.
    I heard the machine make a dreadful noise
    On that awful afternoon.

6. I had to be there at 3 o'clock.
    I knocked very loudly at the door.
    I walked inside and I sat down.
    I trembled as I waited there.
    I heard the machine make a dreadful noise.

    I went next door when I heard the bell.
    I went next door when I heard the bell.
    I went next door when I heard the bell
    On that awful afternoon.

7. I had to be there at 3 o'clock.
    I knocked very loudly at the door.
    I walked inside and I sat down.
    I trembled as I waited there.
    I heard the machine make a dreadful noise.
    I went next door when I heard the bell.

    I opened my mouth and he poked around.
    I opened my mouth and he poked around.
    I opened my mouth and he poked around
    On that awful afternoon.

53

8. I had to be there at 3 o'clock.
I knocked very loudly at the door.
I walked inside and I sat down.
I trembled as I waited there.
I heard the machine make a dreadful noise.
I went next door when I heard the bell.
I opened my mouth and he poked around.

The dentist said "It's all OK." — Hurray.
The dentist said, "It's all OK." — Hurray.
The dentist said, "It's all OK." — Hurray.

1:     On that awful —
2:     Not that awful after all —
1 + 2: That afternoon.

55

A trip to the dentist can have a happy ending. The instruments represent sounds you might hear on such a visit.

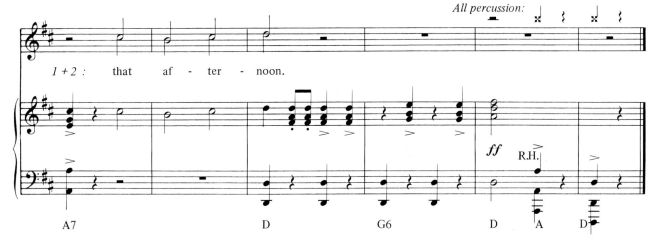

Ideas for performance:

Seven (or more) children are chosen to play the instruments. They sit in the same order as the instruments appear in the song.

They play the rhythm ♩ ♪ ♩ ♪ | ♩ ♪ ▬ as directed in the song.

In the last verse, everyone sings (or shouts!) "Hurray".

Divide the children into two equal groups, 1 and 2, to sing the last nine bars like this:

1 :	On that awful —
2 :	Not that awful after all.——
1 & 2 :	That afternoon.

In this song each verse is extended by adding the sections **A B C D** etc to the previous verse:

Verse 1:	**A** then *Dal Segno* 𝄋
Verse 2:	**A & B** then *Dal Segno* 𝄋
Verse 3:	**A & B & C** then *Dal Segno* 𝄋
	etc.

The section marked **G** leads straight on to the end of the song.

Instruments:

I had to be there at 3 o'clock	Chime bars on the note A
I knocked very loudly at the door	Drum
I walked inside and I sat down	Wood blocks
I trembled as I waited there	Maracas
I heard the machine make a dreadful noise	Cymbals
I went next door when I heard the bell	Triangle
I opened my mouth and he poked around	Finger cymbals

Any number of each instrument may be used.

Abracadabra

1. Have you heard the magic word?
   It's 'Abracadabra'.
   Can you shout and call it out?
   It's 'Abracadabra'.
      Hold your breath and wait for something
      Wonderful and weird —
   Abracadabra,
   And my thumb has disappeared.

2. Have you heard the magic word?
   It's 'Abracadabra'.
   Can you shout and call it out?
   It's 'Abracadabra'.
      Hold your breath and wait for something
      Wonderful and weird —
   Abracadabra,
   And my thumb has appeared.

3. Have you heard the magic word?
   It's 'Abracadabra'.
   Can you shout and call it out?
   It's 'Abracadabra'.
      Hold your breath and wait for something
      Wonderful and weird —
   Abracadabra,
   And my hat has disappeared.

weird.   Ab - ra - cad - ab - ra, and my { thumb has dis - app - eared.
{ thumb has app - eared.

A7   D7   G7   C

4. Have you heard the magic word?
   It's 'Abracadabra'.
   Can you shout and call it out?
   It's 'Abracadabra'.
      Hold your breath and wait for something
      Wonderful and weird —
   Abracadabra,
   And my hat has appeared.

Magic anything away and back again.
With a suitable hideout (behind the piano?) you could even make some children disappear.

Instruments:

No instruments are necessary but you could create some magical sounds at the end of bar 12:

    a glissando on a xylophone;

    a cymbal clash;

    or even a bicycle hooter for a more bizarre effect!

C D E F G A				A B C				C C♯ D E				E F F♯				G A			
Abracadabra				Abracadabra				Abracadabra				Abracadabra				Abracadabra			
①2 3 4				①2 3 4				①2 3 4				①2 3 4				①2 3 4			
C	D	C	C	C	C	C	C	C	C	C	C	E	F	E	E	G	A	G	G
C	D	C	C	C	C	C	C	C	C	C	C	E	F	E	E	G	A	G	G
F	G	E	A	C	B	B	A	C	D	E	C♯	F	F	E	E	A	G	G	A
D	G	C	C	C	B	C	C	D	D	C	C	F♯	F	E	E	A	G	G	G

I Want to Clap My Hands

1. I want to clap my hands.
   I want to tap my head.
      I want to clap my hands —
         tap my head —
   Choose something else instead.

2. I want to pat my thighs.
   I want to tap my head.
      I want to pat my thighs —
         tap my head —
   Choose something else instead.

3. I want to click my fingers.
   I want to tap my head.
      I want to click my fingers —
         tap my head —
   Choose something else instead.

4. I want to stamp my feet.
   I want to tap my head.
      I want to stamp my feet —
         tap my head —
   (last time) We've done everything we said.

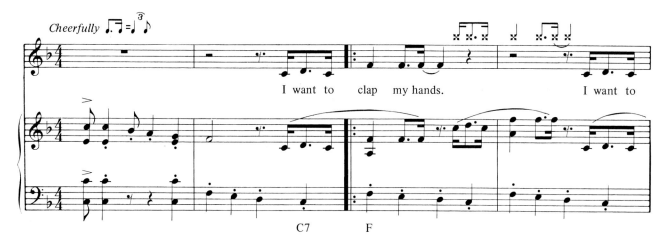

tap my head.   We've done ev - ry - thing we said.

Gm   G♯dim   F   C7   F

Here is a song which incorporates two different actions in each verse.
The second action, "I want to tap my head," remains constant in
every verse.

Ideas for performance:

There are opportunities for soloists here.
Two children could share a verse:

A :	I want to clap my hands –
B :	I want to tap my head –
A :	I want to clap my hands –
B :	Tap my head –
A & B :	Choose something else instead.

Ideas for teachers:

Ask the children to listen to, and then copy these rhythms
before they sing the song:

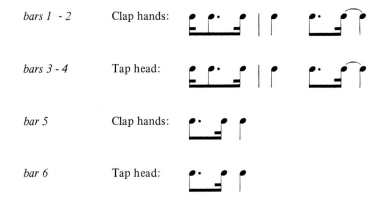

bars 1 - 2   Clap hands:

bars 3 - 4   Tap head:

bar 5   Clap hands:

bar 6   Tap head:

Get in the Bath

1. Get in the bath — (splish splash)
   Get in the bath — (splish splash)
   Get in the bath
   And splash around the tub.

   Get in the bath — (splish splash)
   Get in the bath — (splish splash)
   Get in the bath
   And give yourself a scrub.

   Wash your eyes and ears
       and neck and nose,
   Wash your arms and shoulders
       and knees and toes.

2. Pull out the plug — (glug glug)
   Pull out the plug — (glug glug)
   Pull out the plug
   Away the water goes.

   Pull out the plug — (glug glug)
   Pull out the plug — (glug glug)
   Pull out the plug
   And down the hole it flows.

   Dry your eyes and ears
       and neck and nose,
   Dry your arms and shoulders
       and knees and toes.

   Get into bed.
   Get into bed.

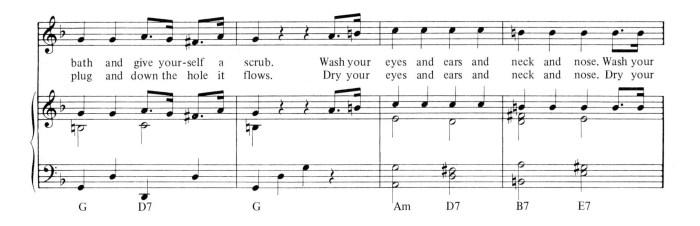

bath and give your-self a scrub. Wash your eyes and ears and neck and nose. Wash your
plug and down the hole it flows. Dry your eyes and ears and neck and nose. Dry your

G   D7   G   Am   D7   B7   E7

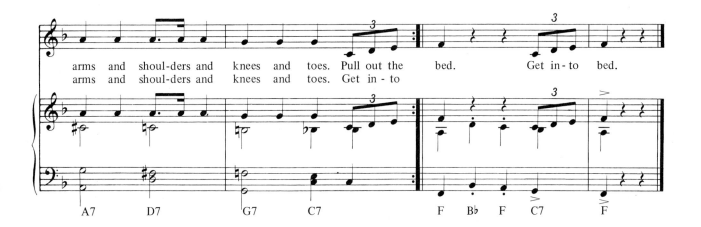

arms and shoul-ders and knees and toes. Pull out the bed. Get in-to bed.
arms and shoul-ders and knees and toes. Get in-to

A7   D7   G7   C7   F   Bb   F   C7   F

Ideas for performance:

Choose a small group of children to say:
"Splish splash" and "glug glug".
Everyone mimes washing and drying.

Would You Like to Sing a Song

1. Would you like to sing a song?
   Yes, I'd like to sing a song.
   Would you like to sing along?
   Yes, I'd like to sing along.
   If you'd like to sing a song then sing along.

2. Would you like to clap a song?
   Yes, I'd like to clap a song.
   Would you like to clap along?
   Yes, I'd like to clap along.
   If you'd like to clap a song then clap along.

3. Would you like to tap a song?
   Yes, I'd like to tap a song.
   Would you like to tap along?
   Yes, I'd like to tap along.
   If you'd like to tap a song then tap along.

4. Would you like to ting a song?
   Yes, I'd like to ting a song.
   Would you like to ting along?
   Yes, I'd like to ting along.
   If you'd like to ting a song then ting along.

long?   If you'd like to sing a   song then sing   a - long.

Yes, I'd like to like to sing a - long.

4
Am   D7   G   G7   C

la   la   la la   la   la la   la la   la

la   la   la la   la   la la   la la

8
Cm   G   B7   Em

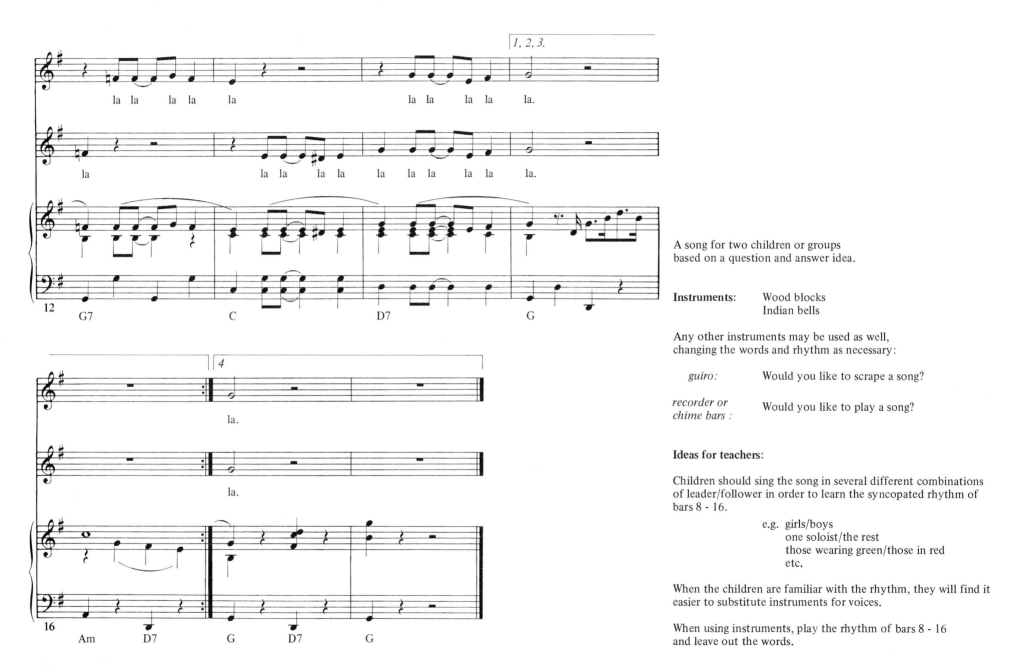

A song for two children or groups based on a question and answer idea.

Instruments: Wood blocks
Indian bells

Any other instruments may be used as well, changing the words and rhythm as necessary:

guiro: Would you like to scrape a song?

recorder or chime bars :   Would you like to play a song?

Ideas for teachers:

Children should sing the song in several different combinations of leader/follower in order to learn the syncopated rhythm of bars 8 - 16.

    e.g. girls/boys
       one soloist/the rest
       those wearing green/those in red
       etc.

When the children are familiar with the rhythm, they will find it easier to substitute instruments for voices.

When using instruments, play the rhythm of bars 8 - 16 and leave out the words.

My Face

1. I've got a nose in the middle of my face,
   My ears are at the side.
   I've got eyes on the right and the left
   And a mouth that opens wide.

   I can twitch my nose.
   I can wiggle my ears at the side.
   I can blink my eyes.
   I can open my mouth very wide.

2. I've got a nose in the middle of my face,
   My ears are at the side.
   I've got eyes on the right and the left
   And a mouth that opens wide.

   I can sniff with my nose.
   I can listen with my ears at the side.
   I can see with my eyes.
   I can sing with my mouth very wide — oh —

3. I've got a nose in the middle of my face,
   My ears are at the side.
   I've got eyes on the right and the left
   And a mouth that opens wide.

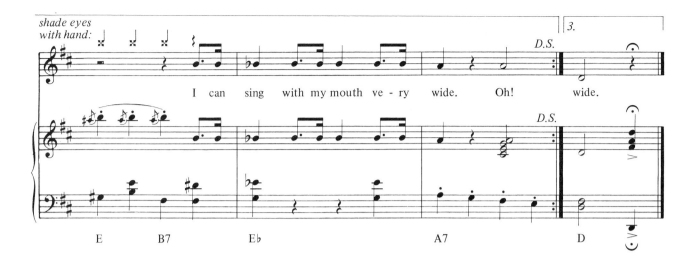

Face and hands are kept busy throughout this song.

Ideas for performance:

In the first section, the children point to each
feature on their face as they sing about it.
In each of the two middle sections, the children
perform the actions as directed in the song.

Ideas for teachers:

Teach the specific rhythm for each action before
singing the song.

The teacher can say,

The children copy the words and actions in the
correct rhythm.

Teacher: I can   wig-gle my   ears   at the   side   (wiggle)

The children copy the words and actions.

Here's a Square

Here's a square, a great big square,
You can see them everywhere.
All four of its edges are just the same.

Cubes are made from six of these,
Joined together like this, you see.
You can use it when you play a game.

6 - 5 - 4 - 3 - 2 - 1
Can you see what they've become?
6 - 5 - 4 - 3 - 2 - 1
It's a dice so start your fun.

Here's a square, a great big square,
You can see them everywhere.
All four of its edges are just the same.

Cubes are made from six of these,
Joined together like this, you see.
You can use it when you play a game.

You can use it when you play a game. 6 5 4 3 2 1

B♭ Gm C F B♭ C Am D7

Can you see what they've be - come? 6 5 4 3 2 1 It's a dice so

Gm C F F7 B♭ C Am D7 Gm

Coda

start your fun. You can use it when you play a game.

Coda

C7 B♭ Gm C7 F

A brief mathematical lesson in solid shapes.

Ideas for performance:

Use a large net of a cube. Mark the dots as on a dice.

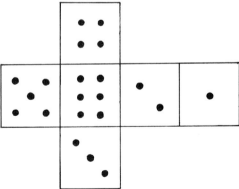

The cube can be formed as the children sing,
"Joined together like this".

71

Five Yellow Butterflies

1. Five yellow butterflies
   Fluttering by;
   One yellow butterfly
   Gave a sigh:
   "I'd like to flutter
   Right up to the sky".
   So that yellow butterfly
   Fluttered high
   And the other four butterflies
   Waved goodbye.

2. Four yellow butterflies
   Fluttering by;
   One yellow butterfly
   Gave a sigh:
   "I'd like to flutter
   Right up to the sky".
   So that yellow butterfly
   Fluttered high
   And the other three butterflies
   Waved goodbye.

sky".   So   that   yel-low butt-er-fly   flutt-ered high and the   oth-er

1. four butt-er- flies
2. three butt-er- flies
3. two butt-er- flies
4. one butt-er- fly

Am   F   Em   F   D9   Em   Am7

waved good - bye.   flutt - ered   high and there   weren't   an-y butt-er-flies to   wave good - bye.

Dm7 G   C   F   D9   Em   Am7   Dm7 G   C

A song in the familiar 'Ten green bottles' mould.

Ideas for performance:

Here is an opportunity for a solo singer in each verse:

"I'd like to flutter
Right up to the sky".

Choose a soloist or a small group of children to make a "fluttering high" effect by playing an ascending scale on a glockenspiel. Pause on the third beat of bar 7, if necessary, to give them extra time.

3. Three yellow butterflies
    Fluttering by;
    One yellow butterfly
    Gave a sigh:
    "I'd like to flutter
    Right up to the sky".
    So that yellow butterfly
    Fluttered high
    And the other two butterflies
    Waved goodbye.

4. Two yellow butterflies
    Fluttering by;
    One yellow butterfly
    Gave a sigh:
    "I'd like to flutter
    Right up to the sky".
    So that yellow butterfly
    Fluttered high
    And the other one butterfly
    Waved goodbye.

5. One yellow butterfly
    Fluttering by;
    One yellow butterfly
    Gave a sigh:
    "I'd like to flutter
    Right up to the sky".
    So that yellow butterfly
    Fluttered high
    And there weren't any butterflies
    To wave goodbye.

73

Things for Fingers

1. Wiggle your fingers in the air;
   Wiggle them here and wiggle them there.

   > Thumbs and fingers, nails and palms,
   > You find your hands at the ends
   > of your arms.

2. Stretch your fingers straight and tall;
   First bend one, then bend them all.

   > Thumbs and fingers, nails and palms,
   > You find your hands at the ends
   > of your arms.

3. Point up high and point down low;
   Point to your eye and point to your toe.

   > Thumbs and fingers, nails and palms,
   > You find your hands at the ends
   > of your arms.

4. Twiddle your thumbs, now hide them away;
   Twiddle them back the other way.

   > Thumbs and fingers, nails and palms,
   > You find your hands at the ends
   > of your arms.

5. One, two, three, four, five, six, seven,
   Eight, nine, ten, but no eleven.

   > Thumbs and fingers, nails and palms,
   > You find your hands at the ends
   >   of your arms.

(faster)

6. Wiggle your fingers in the air;
   Wiggle them here and wiggle them there.

   > Thumbs and fingers, nails and palms,
   > You find your hands at the ends
   >   of your arms.

THINGS FOR FINGERS

Wiggle your fingers in the air;

Wiggle them here

and wiggle them there.

Thumbs

and fingers,

nails

and palms

you find your hands at the ends of your arms.

thumbs and fingers,

nails and palms,

You find your hands at the ends of your arms.

Rum-Tiddly-Um-Tum

1. Listen to us play the tambourine:
   Listen to us play the tambourine:

   > We can play anything all day long
   > While we're singing this song.

2. Listen to us play the wood blocks:
   Listen to us play the wood blocks:
   > We can play anything all day long
   > While we're singing this song.

3. Listen to us play the drum:
   Listen to us play the drum:

   > We can play anything all day long
   > While we're singing this song.

76

an - y-thing all day long while we're sing - ing this song.

Em Dm G7 C F G C

Here's that well known rhythm:

Instruments: Tambourine
                Wood blocks
                Drum
Use other instruments as well, changing the words and rhythm as necessary:

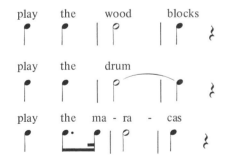

play   the   wood   blocks

play   the   drum

play   the   ma - ra - cas

Ideas for performance:

Give two soloists or small groups tambourines. They sing "Listen to us play the tambourine", then

one soloist plays:

and the other soloist replies:

Both groups sing the last 8 bars, with the instruments playing in bar 22 as written.

Ideas for teachers:

Practise the rhythm

with the children as a question and answer before you sing the song.
Use body sounds (clap hands, click fingers, etc.) before going on to use instruments.

You Can Do It

You can do it —
You can do it —
You can do it if you really try.
    You can meet that challenge,
    Beat that challenge,
    If you really try.
And when you've succeeded you'll feel
    Nine feet high.

1. Sums are hard with all that dividing,
    Adding makes me feel like hiding,
    I just want to take it all away.
    Multiplying's even worse,
    It makes me want to scream and curse,
    But then I hear a little voice inside me say:

    Chorus

2. I can't get my spelling right
    And who decides that site and sight
    Are spelt quite different
        though they sound the same?
    If we say "I saw two mice"
    Then why not say "I saw two hice"?
    But then I hear a little voice deep down exclaim:

    Chorus

78

nine feet high.

1. Sums are hard with all that di - vi - ding.
2. I can't get my spell - ing right and
3. When I'm swim - ming in the wat - er,

E   A7   D   D

Add - ing makes me feel like hi - ding, I just want to take it all a - way.
who de - cides that site and sight are spelt quite diff - 'rent though they sound the same?
ev - en though I know I ought to kick my legs that sink - ing feel - ing's there.

Mult - ip - ly - ing's ev - en worse, it makes me want to
If we say 'I saw two mice', then why not say 'I
Then I feel my head go un - der, that's when I be -

D7   G   G♯dim   F♯m

3. When I'm swimming in the water
   Even though I know I ought to
   Kick my legs, that sinking feeling's there.
   Then I feel my head go under,
   That's when I begin to wonder
   If I'll hear a little voice in me declare:

You can do it —
You can do it —
You can do it if you really try.
   You can meet that challenge,
   Beat that challenge,
   If you really try.
And when you've completed it,
Defeated and repeated it,
You'll feel so high you'll want to touch the sky.

scream and   curse,   but   then I hear a lit - tle   voice   in - side me   say:

saw   two   hice'?   but   then I hear a lit - tle   voice   deep down ex - claim:

gin   to won-der   If I'll hear a lit - tle   voice   in me de - clare:

B7   E7   A7

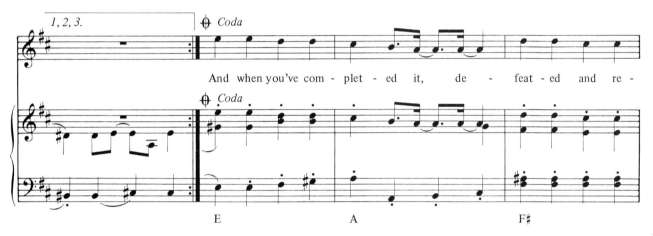

1, 2, 3.   *Coda*

And when you've com - plet - ed it,   de - feat - ed and re -

Coda

E   A   F♯

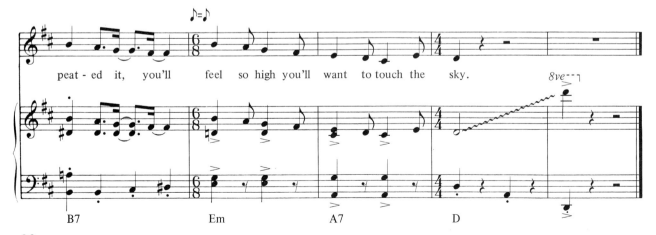

peat - ed it, you'll   feel so high you'll want to touch the sky.

B7   Em   A7   D

A challenging but rewarding song for older children

80

Don't Wake the Baby

1. I was riding on my bike
   As quietly as I could.
   Trying not to wake the baby,
   Trying to be good.

   > When all of a sudden —
   > The bicycle bell rang loud and clear —
   > oh dear —

   > Sh sh — you mustn't wake the baby.
   > Sorry I forgot.
   > Sh sh — you mustn't wake the baby.
   > I didn't mean to.
   > Sh sh — you mustn't wake the baby.
   > Sorry I forgot.

2. I was being a brave Red Indian
   As quietly as I could.
   Trying not to wake the baby,
   Trying to be good.

   When all of a sudden —
   > The Indian call rang loud and clear —
   > oh dear —

   > Sh sh — you mustn't wake the baby.
   > Sorry I forgot.
   > Sh sh — you mustn't wake the baby.
   > I didn't mean to.
   > Sh sh — you mustn't wake the baby.
   > Sorry I forgot.

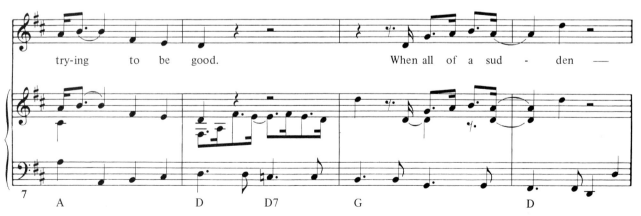

3. I was parking my pedal car
   As quietly as I could.
   Trying not to wake the baby,
   Trying to be good.

   When all of a sudden —
   The hooter just sounded loud and clear —
   oh dear —

Sh sh — you mustn't wake the baby.
   Sorry I forgot.
Sh sh — you mustn't wake the baby.
   I didn't mean to
Sh sh — you mustn't wake the baby.
   Sorry I forgot.

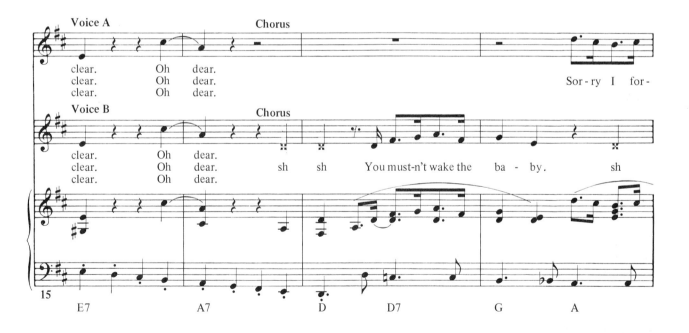

Let this song create a quiet and tranquil atmosphere, so the peace is completely shattered by the percussion effect in bar 11.

Instruments: Bicycle bell (or triangle)
                                Red Indian call – "Ooooh"
                                Pedal car hooter (or cow-bell)
The children will have plenty of ideas for new verses, so make other appropriate noises as well.

Ideas for teachers:

Teach everybody part **B** in the chorus:

"Sh sh – you mustn't wake the baby".

Then divide the class into two and add part **A**:

"Sorry I forgot".

I Would Rather Be

1. When I don't know what else to do
I pretend that I'm not me.
   I can usually think of something
   I would rather be.
I might choose an animal
Or a person or a thing;
   Today I'll be a rattlesnake —
   Now listen to me sing.

2. When I don't know what else to do
I pretend that I'm not me.
   I can usually think of something
   I would rather be.
I might choose an animal
Or a person or a thing;
   Today I'll be a telephone —
   Now listen to me sing.

3. When I don't know what else to do
   I pretend that I'm not me.
     I can usually think of something
     I would rather be.
   I might choose an animal
   Or a person or a thing;
     Today I'll be a fireman —
     Now listen to me sing.

4. When I don't know what else to do
   I pretend that I'm not me.
     I can usually think of something
     I would rather be.
   (last time) We have chosen animals
   And people and things;
     Today we've been a fireman
     and a telephone
     and a rattlesnake —
   Now listen to us sing.

day we've been a   fire-man and a   tel-e-phone and a   rat-tle-snake; now

86

This song has a cumulative effect so everyone needs to stay awake.

Instruments: Scraper
Indian bells
Hand bell
Use any number of each instrument

Ideas for performance:

Choose three soloists or three small groups to play the scraper, Indian bells, and hand bell.

Add as many "animals, people or things" as necessary until everyone has an instrument to play and a character to represent.

Each character will need an extra four bars of piano accompaniment.
The chords D D#dim Em A7 work well.

Verse 1:   The rattlesnake plays.

Verse 2:   The telephone plays,
then the rattlesnake.

Verse 3:   The fireman plays,
then the telephone,
then the rattlesnake.

Please and Thank You

"Please" and "Thank you",
Little words, but so important.

If you use them wherever you go
People'll smile and tell you
what you want to know.

"Please" and "Thank you",
Little words, but so important.

Don't you know that everyone agrees on
"Thank you" and "Please".

88

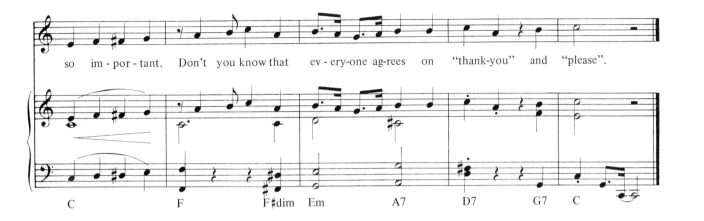

so im - por - tant. Don't you know that ev - ery-one ag-rees on "thank-you" and "please".

C   F   F♯dim Em   A7   D7   G7 C

Ideas for performance:

Choose two soloists or two small groups to sing
"Please" and "Thank you"
each time those words come up in the song.

Tuned percussion parts

C D E F F♯ G A

Please and thank you

① 2 ③ 4

C	G	C	A
D	G	C	C
F	F	E	A
D	D	G	G
G	G		
C	G	C	A
D	G	C	C
F	F♯	G	A
D	G	C	C

A B C

Please and thank you

① 2 ③ 4

C	B	C	C
C	B	C	C
C	C	B	A
C	C	B	B
B	B		
C	B	C	C
C	B	C	C
C	C	B	A
C	B	C	C

C C♯ D D♯

Please and thank you

① 2 ③ 4

C	D♯	C	C
C	D	C	C
C	C	D	C♯
C	C	D	D
D	D		
C	D♯	C	C
C	D	C	C
C	D♯	D	C♯
C	D	C	C

E F F♯

Please and thank you

① 2 ③ 4

E	F	E	E
F	F	E	E
F	F	E	E
F♯	F♯	F	F
F	F		
E	F	E	E
F	F	E	E
F	F♯	E	E
F♯	F	E	E

G A

Please and thank you

① 2 ③ 4

G	G	G	G
A	G	G	G
A	A	G	G
A	A	G	G
G	G		
G	G	G	G
A	G	G	G
A	A	G	G
A	G	G	G

What Will You Do Today?

1. What do you feel like doing today?
   What do you feel like doing today?
   Choose anything that'll make you happy —
   What will you do today?

   > I'd like to do some jumping today,
   > I'd like to do some jumping today,
   > That's what I'll choose to make me happy
   > That's what I'll do today.

2. What do you feel like doing today?
   What do you feel like doing today?
   Choose anything that'll make you happy —
   What will you do today?

   > I'd like to do some creeping today,
   > I'd like to do some creeping today,
   > That's what I'll choose to make me happy
   > That's what I'll do today.

3. What do you feel like doing today?
   What do you feel like doing today?
   Choose anything that'll make you happy —
   What will you do today?

   > I'd like to do some somersaults today,
   > I'd like to do some somersaults today,
   > That's what I'll choose to make me happy
   > That's what I'll do today.

I'd like to do some jump-ing to-day, That's what I'll choose to make me hap-py;

D   Bm   Em   A7   D   B7   Em   Fdim

That's what I'll do to-day.

D   A7   D   D7   G   Em   Am   D7   G   Em

1, 2, 3, etc. | *Last time*

pp   *f*

Am   D7   G D7 G   C   C♯dim   G   D7   G   A7   G

You can choose anything to make you happy:

"I'd like to do some jumping today . . .

clap my hands today . . .

be a giant today . . .

ride on a bus today . . .

play the maracas today . . .

eat some spaghetti today . . ."

Ideas for performance:

A soloist or small group chooses an activity.
Everyone else sings the question,
and the soloist sings the answer.
The last eight bars accompany the activity.

Place the Place

1. Listen to the dogs in Barking bark,
   If they like you they will wag their tails.
   > Look at all the swans in Swansea glide,
   > Buy an ox at an Oxford sales.
   But even if you're searching high and wide
   You won't find a whale in Wales.

   > See the sights of every site you see,
   > Wonder how it got its name.
   > Find a map and spot the spot;
   > Place the place is the name of the game.

2. Hampshire is the place for a slice of ham,
   Be polite and don't forget to say please.
   > Peel all the peel off an orange in Peel;
   > Go to Cheddar if you want some cheese.
   But Chippenham's the best place for a meal
   Of chips'n'ham with peas.

   > See the sights of every site you see,
   > Wonder how it got its name.
   > Find a map and spot the spot;
   > Place the place is the name of the game.

Tuned percussion parts (chorus only)

A song for older children with an interest in maps.
The first verse refers to animal life, the second to food.

Children will find an endless list of places
with interesting names.

What Are You Wearing?

1. What are you wearing today?
   What are you wearing today?
      Let's choose the people with buttons
      To have their turn to play.

2. What are you wearing today?
   What are you wearing today?
      Let's choose the people with red on
      To have their turn to play.

3. What are you wearing today?
   What are you wearing today?
      Let's choose the people with socks on
      To have their turn to play.

4. What are you wearing today?
   What are you wearing today?
      Let's choose the people with stripes on
      To have their turn to play.

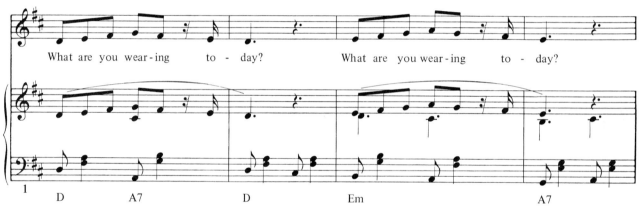

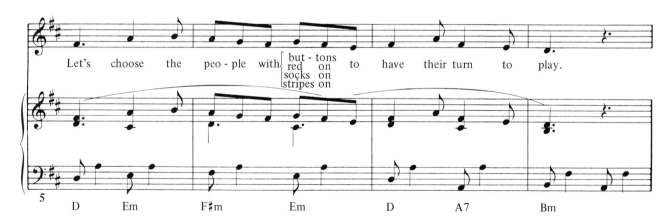

94

Everyone has a turn, whatever they are wearing.

Instruments: Everyone has an instrument.

Ideas for performance:

Name any article of clothing in bar 6,
and those children who are wearing it play in bars 9 - 16.

Say: but - tons   but - tons

and play:

Say: red red   red red

and play:

Choose anything: a colour; type of material;
a print; or a smile!